Dedication

LuLu is dedicated to our grandchildren, Lauren Gallagher Bradley and Sophie Camille Leigh Yager.

Acknowledgements

We wish to acknowledge Carol Chapman for her ideas, Angela Palmer for her dance expertise and Patrick Looney for his technical assistance.

Finally, we want to acknowledge Finn and Aidan for finding *LuLu* in our woods on Little Woahink Lake.

The Library of Congress # 2013916036
ISBN-13: 978-1492277187
ISBN-10: 1492277185

LuLu... the dancing snail

By Connie Strome Bradley

Illustrations by Carol Johnson Unser

 Sutton Shores Press

"Mother," said *LuLu*, the little snail, "When I grow up I want to be a famous dancer."

Mother was surprised and asked,

"*LuLu*, What kind of famous dancer do you want to be?"

"I don't know!" said *LuLu*,

Could I try some dances?"

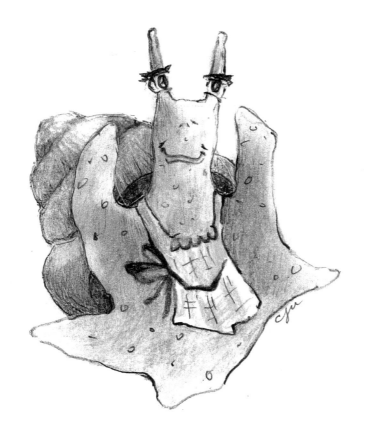

Mother enrolled *LuLu*

in Tap Dancing lessons.

LuLu learned to toe

tap and brush step.

LuLu, the little snail

cried "Boo Hoo, I don't want to be a tap dancer.

I don't want to make noise when I dance."

Tap Dancing LuLu

Mother enrolled *LuLu* in

Square Dancing lessons.

LuLu learned to swing

your partner and

do sa do. *LuLu*, the little

snail cried "Boo Hoo,

I don't want to be a square dancer.

I want to twirl and jump."

Square Dancing LuLu

Mother enrolled *LuLu* in

Ballroom Dancing lessons.

LuLu learned the Waltz,

Foxtrot and promenade.

LuLu, the little snail cried

"Boo Hoo, I don't want to dance with animals."

Ballroom Dancing LuLu

Mother enrolled *LuLu* in

Hula Dancing lessons. She

learned to tell a story

with her hands and

hip movements. She

wore a lei and a grass skirt. *LuLu*,

the little snail cried "Boo Hoo, I don't want to be a

hula dancer.

I don't like ukulele music."

Hula Dancing LuLu

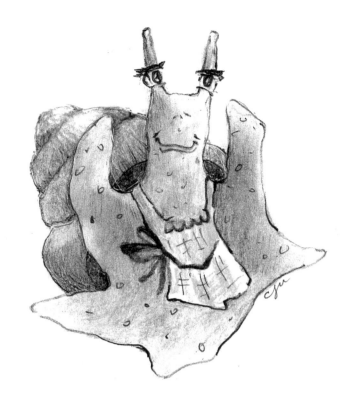

Mother enrolled

LuLu in Country

Line Dancing lessons.

Mother bought her

boots and a hat. She

learned the grapevine

and the Boot Scootin' Boogie. *LuLu*, the little snail

cried "Boo Hoo, I don't want to be a line dancer.

My boots hurt my feet."

Country Line Dancing LuLu

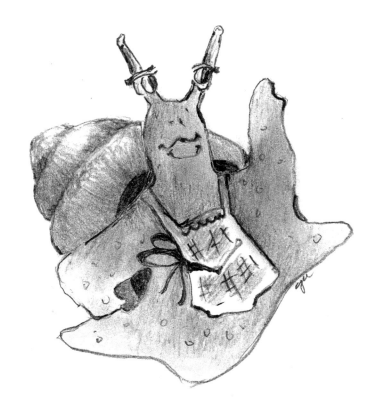

Mother enrolled

LuLu in Salsa

Dancing lessons.

LuLu learned the

break step and

the Cuban. *LuLu*, the

little snail cried "Boo Hoo, I don't want to be a

salsa dancer. It makes me hungry."

Salsa Dancing LuLu

Mother enrolled *LuLu* in

Irish Dancing lessons. She

learned to do the

step dance.

LuLu, the little snail

cried "Boo Hoo, I don't want to Irish dance.

I want to dance with my arms and legs."

Irish Dancing LuLu

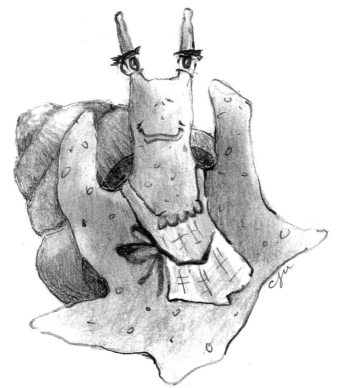

Mother enrolled *LuLu*

in Folk Dancing lessons.

She learned the Hokey

Pokey and how to

put her left foot in

and left foot out.

LuLu, the little snail cried

"Boo Hoo, I don't want to be a folk dancer.

I don't want to know what it's all about."

Folk Dancing LuLu

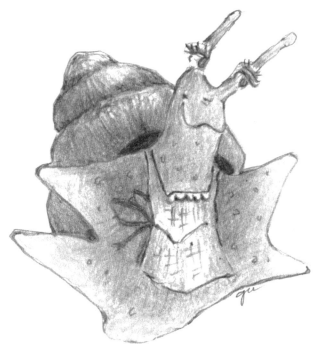

Mother asked *LuLu*,

"What kind of famous dancer

do you want to be?"

LuLu said, "I want

to be a ballerina!"

Mother enrolled *LuLu* in

Ballet Dancing lessons.

Mother bought

LuLu a pink bag and ballet slippers.

She learned to plie, releve' and pirouette.

She was dancing with her arms and

legs, her slippers didn't hurt her feet,

there was no ukulele music,

and she wasn't hungry.

She twirled and jumped.

LuLu, the little snail, never

Boo Hoo'd when she

wore her tutu!

Life is a ballet 'Let's Dance'

For more about LuLu and other snails

Glossary of *LuLu's* Dances

TAP DANCING:

Tap dancing is an exciting form of dance in which dancers wear special shoes equipped with metal taps. Tap dancers use their feet like drums to create rhythmic patterns and timely beats.

SQUARE DANCING:

Square dancing is a fast-paced, lively type of folk dance. It is a fun form involving social interaction between several dancers, usually four couples arranged in a square. A 'caller' guides the the dancers through a sequence of steps in time to the music.

BALLROOM DANCING:

There are many styles of ballroom dancing, including slower dances like the waltz with sweeping movements and stylish poses to the fast-moving swing, with lots of spins and lots of fun. Ballroom dancers have partners to dance with.

HULA DANCING:

Hula is a type of dance developed by Polynesians in the islands of Hawaii. Hula dancers may be women or men. The dance is accompanied by a chant, or song. Each movement has a specific meaning, especially hand movements.

COUNTRY LINE DANCING:

Country line dancing is a popular style of dance in which a group of people performs a sequence of steps in unison while facing each other in rows. Women tend to line dance while holding their hands in fists at waist level, while men often prefer to line dance with their hands in their pockets or resting in their belts.

SALSA DANCING:

Salsa is a very energetic Latin dance, complete with spins, sharp movements and crisp turns. Couples dance to fast rhythms and loud, upbeat music.

IRISH STEP DANCING:

Irish dance is a type of traditional dance form that originated in Ireland. Irish step dancing is known for its rapid leg movements and stationary body with arms held stiff and straight at the dancer's sides.

FOLK DANCING:

Folk dance reflects the traditional life of the people of a certain country or region. Folk dancing originated in the 18th century to distinguish dance forms of common people from those of the upper classes. The steps of folk dances are passed through generations, rarely being changed.

BALLET DANCING:

Ballet dance is a very formal and strict type of performance dance. It originated in 16th and 17th century France, and further developed in England, Italy and Russia. Ballet dancers are highly skilled and usually perform to classical music. In order to become a good ballet performer, a dancer must be dedicated to hard work and practice long hours.

Information about *LuLu* and other snails.

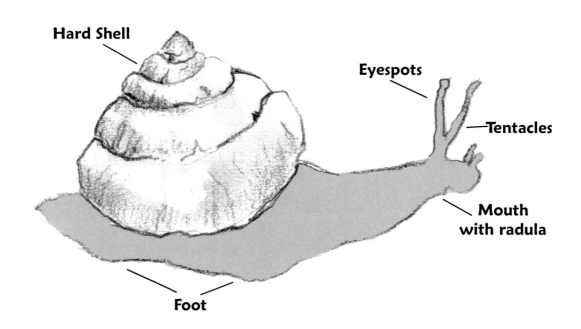

Hard Shell

Eyespots

Tentacles

Mouth with radula

Foot

Snail Facts

Kingdom:	Animalia	Number of Species:	1,000
Phylum:	Mollusca	Average Lifespan:	1 - 20 years
Class:	Gastropoda	Conservation Status:	Least Concern
Order:	Achatinoidea	Color:	Black. Brown, Yellow, Tan
Common Name:	Snail	Skin Type:	Shell
Scientific Name:	Achatinoidea	Favorite Food:	Leaves
Found:	Worldwide	Habitat:	Well-vegetated areas
Diet:	Herbivore	Average Litter Size:	200
Size (L):	0.5cm - 80cm (0.2in - 32in)	Distinctive Features:	Armored shell with long, thin eye stems
Weight:	0.01kg - 18kg (0.02lbs - 40lbs)		

Lulu, the dancing snail is not a real snail, but a wonderful way we can imagine a little snail learning something new, exciting and sometimes hard. But she keeps on trying until she finds a way to be happy.

The snail is a soft-bodied animal that is basically a head with a flattened foot. The soft body is protected by a hard shell, which the snail retreats into when alarmed. These animals are found worldwide in the oceans, in the fresh water and on land.

Like, LuLu, real snails that live in the water have eyespots at the base of their tentacles; land snails have eyespots located at the tips of their larger tentacles, instead of closer to the heads.

Most snails eat living and rotting plants. They eat using a radule, a rough tongue-like organ that has thousands of denticles. Denticles are like tiny, tiny teeth.

Snails move slowly by crawling across the ground along their large, flat foot. The common garden snail is the slowest moving animal! The largest land snail is the Giant African Snail. It is over 15 inches long and weighs about 2 pounds.

Made in United States
Orlando, FL
17 May 2022

17969664R00020